THE
COBBLER'S
~REWARD~

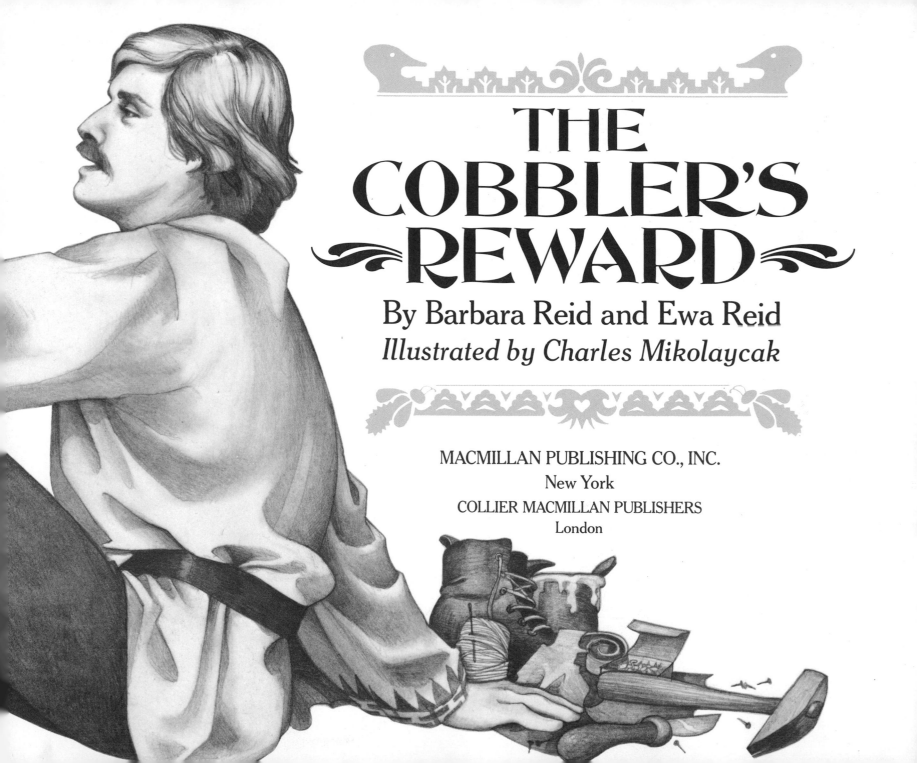

THE COBBLER'S REWARD

By Barbara Reid and Ewa Reid

Illustrated by Charles Mikolaycak

MACMILLAN PUBLISHING CO., INC.

New York

COLLIER MACMILLAN PUBLISHERS

London

Macmillan Publishing Co., Inc.
866 Third Avenue, New York, N.Y. 10022
Collier Macmillan Canada, Ltd.
Printed in the United States of America
Typographic design by Ben Birnbaum.

10 9 8 7 6 5 4 3 2 1

LIBRARY OF CONGRESS CATALOGING IN PUBLICATION DATA
Reid, Barbara.   The cobbler's reward.
SUMMARY: A cobbler's kindness to animals comes
back to him when he attempts to outwit a witch
and win a beautiful bride.
[1. Folklore—Poland]   I. Reid, Ewa Malewicz,
joint author.   II. Mikolaycak, Charles.   III. Title.
PZ8.1.R275Co 1978   [398.2]   78-4638
ISBN 0-02-775800-1

For Jamie and Stephen
Marek and Danusia
Heidi, Ben and Chris

—B.R. and E.R.

There was once a young cobbler who lived in a village outside great Piska Forest in Old Poland. His name was Janek Dobry, which means John, the Kind One. He was as friendly as the sparrows that chirped outside his clay hut all winter when the storks and swallows had flown to southern lands.

But there came a time when there were no more shoes and boots to mend in that village. Janek became very poor. So one morning he decided to travel from town to town seeking work. He put his needle, scissors and thread and a few loaves of black bread in his knapsack and set out on a path through the dark forest.

"I'll have shoes to mend
And money to spend,"

Janek sang as he walked.

Before long Janek saw a trampled ant hill beside the path. Thousands of ants scurried about it, carrying grains of sand and pine needles. Surrounding their scattered nest were huge bear tracks. A bear had clawed the nest, searching for ant eggs to eat.

Janek watched the ants putting together the grains of sand and pine needles which the bear had tossed in all directions. He shook his head with pity and thought: Why, the sun will set a hundred times before the poor insects have a nest!

"Let me build your nest!" he said to the ants. Then he took off his cap, and with it he brushed the sand and pine needles into a cone-shaped pile.

When she saw her nest, the queen ant came up and said: "Thank you, good man! If you ever need us, we will come to help you!"

What can the tiny ants do for me? thought Janek. But he thanked the insect for her offer and went on his way.

After a while the forest ended and he came to a meadow with a tall oak tree. Bees hummed loudly as they swarmed around the tree. A bear had been there also, searching for honey to eat.

Janek looked about. In a hollow of the tree trunk he saw a broken beehive. The wax combs which the bees had built lay on the ground, and Janek thought: Why, the moon will rise a hundred nights before the poor bees have a hive!

Again his heart stirred with pity. "Let me build your hive!" he said to the bees. Then he put the wax combs back in the hollow of the tree.

When she saw her hive, the queen bee flew up and said: "Thank you, kind man! If you ever are in trouble, we will come to help you!"

How can the small bees help me? Janek asked himself. But he thanked the queen bee for her offer and went on his way.

It was evening now and the young cobbler was tired. The setting sun was staining the sky rose when he came to a lake. Wild ducks were nesting on the grassy bank. That will be a fine place to sleep! Janek thought and walked toward the ducks.

But as soon as the ducks saw Janek, they hid in the reeds and water lilies. They thought he was a hunter who had come to kill them.

Janek cried: "Come back, pretty ducks. I have bread for you!" Then he took some bread out of his knapsack and threw pieces in the water.

The ducks paddled out of their hiding places and ate the bread. No one had brought them food before, and when they had finished, the oldest drake swam up and said: "Thank you, kind man! You chose to feed rather than hunt us. If bad luck should ever befall you, we will come to help you!"

What can the small ducks do for me? Janek thought, but he thanked the drake for his offer. Then he ate some bread, put his knapsack under his head and went to sleep.

In the morning he went on. Soon he saw the tall tower of a castle rising from the plain. That is the town of Kolno sure enough, Janek thought, so he walked toward it.

Now he saw fields of flax and barley rippling in the sun. He passed the wooden huts of peasants, with the savory smells of cabbage and *kielbasa* coming from the windows. He saw large brick houses and stables and inns.

I don't have a broken penny by my soul, but soon I will be rich, thought Janek.

At last he reached a busy market square where the castle stood. A crowd of people were gazing at its great stone tower.

"Tell me what you are looking at," Janek said to a man with a bundle of firewood.

"We hope the beautiful maiden will come to the window," the man replied.

"She is imprisoned by the old witch," said a second man, putting down his sack of potatoes. "Poor thing, she can't eat or sleep or even call to the birds without asking the witch. No one has been able to free her—not even our Prince and Princess. The witch has the power of death over everyone in Kolno!"

Then the first man said, "Whoever marries the maiden can free her from the witch. But first he must perform two tasks and solve a riddle. And no one has succeeded so far."

"I'm quick at tasks and clever at riddles," said Janek.

"Don't think of it," said the man, seeing he was new to the town. "If you try and fail, the witch will make you lose your handsome head! Kings from far away have wanted to free the maiden. So have knights and wealthy merchants. They could not do the tasks or guess the riddle, and they all died."

"I still want to try," said Janek.

He walked over a drawbridge and knocked on the castle's door. It flew open and the witch stepped out. She was dressed in black and had small black eyes like glittering buttons. Her voice was a hoarse croak. She gave him a cunning look and asked:

"Why do you knock?
What do you want?"

"I want to marry the maid in the tower," Janek replied. The witch's eyes became piercing. She said:

"If you can quickly do
The first and second task,
And then correctly guess
The riddle I shall ask,
Then you'll marry her!"

Janek trembled with fear but he said, "Tell me what I must do!"

"Follow me!" exclaimed the witch.

Janek stepped inside the door. It closed behind him like a thunderclap.

"Come!" said the witch in her harsh voice. Then she led him down a long hall to a large, dark room. It had seven doors and a window covered with iron bars. It was empty except for a heavy bag on the floor. She looked at Janek with her sly eyes and said:

"Here is a bag
   Of poppy seed and sand.
   Sort it before dawn
   Creeps over the land.
   If it is not ready when the cock crows,
   I will cut off your head!"

Then she vanished, locking all seven doors.

Janek sat down beside the bag and started to separate the poppy seed from the sand. Soon his eyes blurred and his fingers hurt. Stars covered the iron bars of the window with their frosty light and still the bag was full. He looked at the

tiny piles he had sorted. Why, I could work all year—from spring to spring when the storks fly home—and I couldn't empty this bag! he thought, his eyes filling with tears.

Suddenly he saw that between the window's bars, then down the wall, crept thousands of ants—a great army led by the queen. They formed a circle around the cobbler, and the queen ant came forward. "We have marched many leagues through forest and plain," she said, "to keep our promise to help you. What is your wish, kind man?"

"Oh, there is no one who can grant my wish," answered the cobbler.

"Tell us what it is," said the queen ant.

"Well," said the cobbler sadly, "the witch has given me this bag. I must sort the poppy seed and sand in it. Unless I do so, I shall die!"

"That is no trouble for us!" said the queen ant. "Empty the bag so we can work!"

Janek emptied the bag on the floor and the ants began to work. "Poppy seed on the right, sand on the left," they said as they separated the seed from the sand into two large piles. By midnight the job was done. "We must go back to our forest now," said the queen ant. "Sleep like a woodchuck in winter, little cobbler." Then the ants marched out of the window.

As soon as the first cock crowed at dawn, the seven doors swung open. The witch burst into the room, astonished

to see the poppy seed and sand neatly sorted and the young cobbler stretching after a good night's sleep. She was furious but she said:

> "Today you have a second task.
> I had a golden key.
> I swam in the lake and dropped it.
> The water is deep as the sea.
> If you do not find it by twilight,
> You will lose your head to me!"

Then she led the cobbler to the door and disappeared.

Janek hurried to the lake. How could he find such a small thing as the golden key? He could not dive to the lake's deep hidden places. His heart sank.

As he was standing there sadly, all at once the oldest drake appeared. "What do you want, dear friend?" the drake asked.

"I want the golden key that the witch dropped in the lake," said Janek. "If I do not find it, she will have my head."

"Do not be anxious, little cobbler," said the drake. "All the ducks will look, all the fish will dive—and we will find your key."

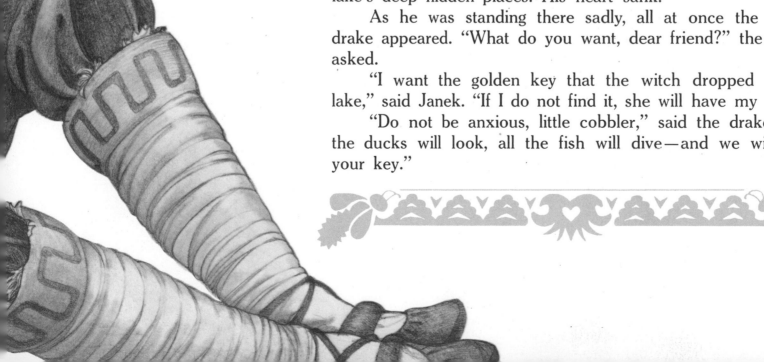

With that the ducks came out from the reeds and water lilies and paddled far into the lake. The water churned white around them as a school of fish swam to the surface. Then the fish dived to the bottom. They darted past shadowy rocks and through waving reeds to the deepest spring that fed the lake. Here, in a crevice of a rock, they saw the golden key gleaming. A fish caught it in his mouth and brought it to the drake. Then the drake took it in his bill and paddled to the shore. He dropped it onto the grass at Janek's feet and said: "Here is your golden key, dear friend!"

Janek could not believe his good luck. "You have saved my life!" he cried with joy.

"It was our turn to help you," the drake replied. "We have kept our promise, little cobbler."

It was nearly twilight when Janek returned to the castle. The witch was waiting at the door. Her eyes shone with a cold, unpleasant light.

"Your task is done. I have found your key!" the cobbler told her, putting it in her hand.

The witch was more furious than ever, but she said:

> "Golden door,
> Golden key,
> Will you perish?
> Will it be me?"

"Come!" she said in her rasping voice. Then she led

Janek down the long hall to the stairway leading to the tower. The cobbler looked up.

"Come!" the witch said again and smiled as she heard his footsteps behind her.

They climbed seven hundred and seventy-seven steps until they reached a golden door set in the wall. The witch opened the door with her golden key.

Janek followed her into a round room with a long window —the very window he had gazed at from the market square. Then he drew in his breath with amazement. Against the wall, on golden chairs, sat nine young maidens. Each had long hair and wore a beautiful blouse, and each had a white veil hiding her face.

"Who are you?" Janek asked, but the maidens did not answer. He turned to the witch.

She watched him closely. Then she laughed and said:

> "This is a riddle—hold your breath—
> Either a wedding or your death.
> In a minute night will fall,
> In a minute day will end.
> Tell me who the maiden is,
> Or I will have your head, my friend!"

Janek went over to the maidens. He gazed at each one, trying to guess who was the prisoner. But the maidens all looked alike. And all remained silent.

I cannot tell one from the other, he thought. How foolish I was to think I could save the maiden! He looked out the window with terror, only to see the red sun sinking over the plain. What can I do? he wondered.

And then through the window, the golden bees entered the room. They flew around it twice, then settled in a ring around the head of the last maiden.

When they had done this, the queen bee flew up to Janek and said, "We knew your wish, dear friend. We flew over forest and plain to keep our promise. This is the maiden you seek!" Then she led the bees out the window.

Janek's heart leaped with happiness. He ran to the last maiden and said, "Now you are free!" Then he turned to the witch. "Old witch, here is the answer to your riddle! Here she is!"

The maiden threw away her veil and flung her arms around the young man's neck. She was as beautiful as the fern flower that blooms once a year in Piska Forest.

When the witch saw this, she was afraid. In the wink of an eye she changed herself to a large black raven, flapped her wings and flew out the window. That was the last anyone saw of her in Kolno.

All week the villagers danced in the streets. The Prince and Princess gave Janek and the maiden the largest wedding the town had ever seen. People came from far and wide, even from the big city of Warsaw, and toasted them with mead and wine. The Princess came with a silver bowl filled with salt. "May your life always have savor," she said, giving the bowl to the maiden. The Prince came with a loaf of bread. "May you never want for bread," he said, giving the bread to Janek. Then they gave them a splendid house and all the money they could spend.

The cobbler's fame spread. He had enough shoes and boots to sew all his life, and so he lived in Kolno with his beloved maiden, happily ever after as the saying goes. The villagers wondered why he disappeared from time to time into the forest, but that was his secret, and the secret of the ants and bees and small creatures who lived there.

The text of this book has been set in a photo version
of fourteen point Cheltenham Medium with Italic. The face
is one of a related group of types designed as a family
by Bertram Goodhue, beginning in 1900, in collaboration
with Ingalls Kimball and his Cheltenham Press in New York.
Titles in the book are set in the capitals of Abbott Old
Style, an example of the Medieval Revival types
fashionable early in this century.